A Silly Littl

MW00941631

ISBN

9781716756023

By Todd R. Burns

A Silly Little Ranch

Dedicated to my loving and hard working wife

Ranch Boss

Diana

By Todd R. Burns

A Silly Little Ranch

There once was a little pig

Who thought she was a chicken

I guess she didn't know, I guess she wasn't thinkin'

Her name is Rosemary

By Todd R. Burns

A Silly Little Ranch

Little Rosemary loved to play

She would run and push and squeak and spin

Even though she was very small

As small as a tennis ball

By Todd R. Burns

A Silly Little Ranch

Once a pig named TJ – ran away and became a stray

Then he came home – a safe little one

So we called him the prodigal son

By Todd R. Burns

A Silly Little Ranch

TJ and Rosemary would run and squeal

And because they lived in the house

Not every day was fun and play

Sometimes they and to study and learn

With a keyboard and a mouse

By Todd R. Burns

A Silly Little Ranch

Then A Silly Little Ranch got some donkeys

Apache and our Charlie Brown

They honk and play most every day

And donkeys never frown

By Todd R. Burns

A Silly Little Ranch

Apache Apache what are you doing

Said Momma about her drink

Go over there and eat the grass

And stop being such an . . .

Donkey

By Todd R. Burns

A Silly Little Ranch

Then we got a mammoth donkey

His name is Mr. Spock

And when you walk right up to him

It can be quite a shock

By Todd R. Burns

A Silly Little Ranch

He is very tall with great big ears

He uses them to hear - and when you talk to him

There is no need to fear

By Todd R. Burns

A Silly Little Ranch

Ranch Boss Diana loves Mr. Spock

And loves to take him for a ride

But it was not always so – don't you know

He used to go and hide

By Todd R. Burns

A Silly Little Ranch

Then came Albert a mustang paint

One early Autumn day

He found new friends at A Silly Little Ranch

And all of them would play

By Todd R. Burns

A Silly Little Ranch

And so Mr. Spock and Albert Tiberius

Became the best of friends

And Albert showed Spock the fun of riding

Where the trail never ends

By Todd R. Burns

A Silly Little Ranch

So one day a girl named Fiona

Whispered in Mr Spock's ear

Would you like to take a ride with me

And Mr Spock smiled with glee

By Todd R. Burns

A Silly Little Ranch

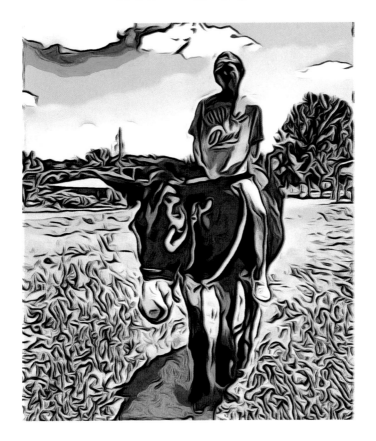

So off they rode

Out to the pasture

On a very special day

By Todd R. Burns

A Silly Little Ranch

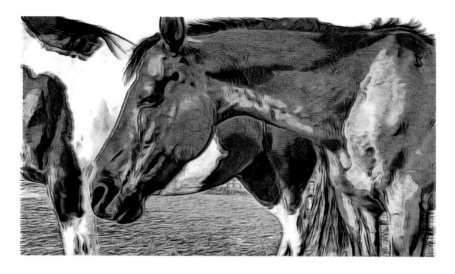

And we had a loving soul

An old horse we named Juniper

And he would pray at the end of the day

Thanking the Lord for the ranch and hay

By Todd R. Burns

A Silly Little Ranch

Now the donkeys continued to play every day

With a ball a rope or a hose

And now and then Spock would play

(next page please)

By Todd R. Burns

A Silly Little Ranch

And they would sock him in the nose

Lol. :)

By Todd R. Burns

A Silly Little Ranch

And A Silly Little Ranch adopted

A herd of little ones

So they would have a home where they could roam

and a place to be loved – tons and tons

By Todd R. Burns

A Silly Little Ranch

And then she was born here on the ranch

Ranch Boss Diana's very special one

Baby Ayasha is her name

Which in Cherokee means Little One

By Todd R. Burns

A Silly Little Ranch

When you meet Ayasha you will see how cute

This little Donkey can be

Watch out Watch out Baby Ayasha

You might be stung by a bee

By Todd R. Burns

A Silly Little Ranch

I may have said Donkeys don't frown

But one Christmas Spock may have done just that

He laid on the ground with maybe a frown

I don't think he liked the Santa hat

By Todd R. Burns

A Silly Little Ranch

Now Momma Cherokee didn't mind at all

She liked her Christmas hat that day

But we had to be careful and take it off

So it did not get full of hay

By Todd R. Burns

A Silly Little Ranch

The Donkey named Walker could be quite a talker

And he whispered to Spock

He said "you look so silly with that hat on your ears"

And they both laughed so hard

Their eyes filled with tears

By Todd R. Burns

A Silly Little Ranch

Buttercup Buttercup

Shes a little bitty baby Buttercup

Buttercup Buttercup

How they loved her so

By Todd R. Burns

A Silly Little Ranch

And soon A Silly Little Ranch had many goats

So many goats they ate the oats

By Todd R. Burns

A Silly Little Ranch

DJ and BB and Brandy

Would play on the hammock

They would swing and bounce and sway

And when they were done in the middle of the day

That is where they all would lay

By Todd R. Burns

A Silly Little Ranch

A pig and a cat

How about that

Sugar and Boo

We love you

By Todd R. Burns

A Silly Little Ranch

Boo and Elvis would swing at the pelvis

When ever Elvis would crow

You ain't nothin' but a swine hog, just eating all the time

Boo did not look amused

By Todd R. Burns

A Silly Little Ranch

And we have some cows

Or maybe highland Coos

This is little baby Scotty

We love to hear him moo

By Todd R. Burns

A Silly Little Ranch

And we have Mr Worf another little bull

And he goes moo and moo until his belly's full

By Todd R. Burns

A Silly Little Ranch

Then along came

Mary Queen of Scots and she was very very large

Nothing to fear because she is so dear

And never will she charge

By Todd R. Burns

A Silly Little Ranch

Here is silly Snowflake

With her best friend Talia too

They love their treats when you come to visit

And you will hear them moo for you

By Todd R. Burns

A Silly Little Ranch

Snowflake Snowflake what are we going to do

You should not moo with a mouth full of oats

You will end up sounding just like the goats

By Todd R. Burns

A Silly Little Ranch

There is Mary again with her head in the oats

She is much to big

But she thinks she's a goat

By Todd R. Burns

A Silly Little Ranch

This is baby Valentine

Born on a special day

If you can guess if you can figure it out

Say it out loud with a great big shout

By Todd R. Burns

A Silly Little Ranch

And she has a little brother who is named Alexander

And she protects him when they are alone

If something is wrong she has to moo

Because she doesn't have a phone

By Todd R. Burns

A Silly Little Ranch

Catch me Valentine if you can

You will have to run very fast

I am Alexander the bull with the speed of light

And daddy will also teach me to fight

By Todd R. Burns

A Silly Little Ranch

And then when it gets so very hot

In the shade we go with dad for a nap

Chewing away the afternoon

Listening to birds as they sing a tune

By Todd R. Burns

A Silly Little Ranch

Now the Highland Coos are very hairy

And like to stand in the pond to keep cool

And with horns like that on a very hot day

I don't think anyone would call them a fool

By Todd R. Burns

A Silly Little Ranch

Have you ever seen a zebra?

Have you ever seen a donkey?

If you mash them up right – you get yourself a zonkey!

By Todd R. Burns

A Silly Little Ranch

Zed the Zonkey is a very gentle friend

You can touch his nose – you can scratch his ears

And you will see him out in the pasture

Before the hayride ends

By Todd R. Burns

A Silly Little Ranch

Penny Penny with a silly smile

Who learned how to ride – and learned how to shake

She loves the attention from all she sees

And Penny Penny loves to please

By Todd R. Burns

A Silly Little Ranch

Little JW loves his Penny

He follows her everywhere

They frolic and play and eat their hay

And live without a care

By Todd R. Burns

A Silly Little Ranch

There's the Duke

It's not a fluke

He thinks he's a giraffe today

By Todd R. Burns

A Silly Little Ranch

And if you look closely at our very big Duke

You might see something that looks like a horse

Not on the land – not one that stands

But the shape of a wild SEA HORSE

By Todd R. Burns

A Silly Little Ranch

Momma kisses Job on the nose

And tells him it's time to go

The kids love to ride – and feel such pride

When Job puts on his show

By Todd R. Burns

A Silly Little Ranch

Leighton loves to ride his Job

To get him ready for his job

To pony the kids around the shop

And Job always knows – where to stop

By Todd R. Burns

A Silly Little Ranch

Phoenix Arizona hiding on the porch

Because he is a little bit shy

But you can see him when you stop over

If you really try

By Todd R. Burns

A Silly Little Ranch

Tuscon Arizona

Who doesn't love that face

He is not so shy and soon you'll see why

He struts around like he owns the place

By Todd R. Burns

A Silly Little Ranch

In the winter Phoenix is fuzzy

And looks so plump and round

In the springtime we trim him to keep him cool

And the hair falls to the ground

By Todd R. Burns

A Silly Little Ranch

Phoenix and Tuscon looking around

For a little bite to eat

They look on the ground where grass can be found

Around their fuzzy feet

By Todd R. Burns

A Silly Little Ranch

And if you have some ducks

And you mix them up with an Alpaca

Something very silly comes out

You end up with AlQauckas

By Todd R. Burns

A Silly Little Ranch

Indian runners stand up straight

And don't mind little Boo

They waddle and quack sound like a laugh

And soon you'll be laughing too

By Todd R. Burns

A Silly Little Ranch

Big Tom the Tortoise looks very large

And looks like a dinosaur

He walks very slow but you should know

He doesn't really roar

By Todd R. Burns

A Silly Little Ranch

Tiny Tim is Big Tom's pal

Together they chill in the shade

Two Tortoise together what could be better

These two boys have it made

By Todd R. Burns

A Silly Little Ranch

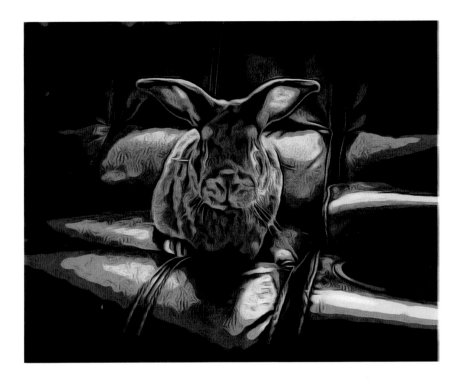

Red Buttons Red Buttons

Watching TV

Hey mom change the channel

Find something for me

By Todd R. Burns

A Silly Little Ranch

A rooster and a bunny

Now that's really funny

In the house watching TV

How wonderful can it be

By Todd R. Burns

A Silly Little Ranch

A boy named Blaze came to visit

A boy who could not see

But with his heart and with his hands and with his feet

Albert knew his soul was sweet

By Todd R. Burns

A Silly Little Ranch

And he rode the horse named Job

At A Silly Little Ranch

All by himself around he went around and around the shop

And when it was finally time to go

He didn't want to stop

By Todd R. Burns

A Silly Little Ranch

Thank you for reading the story of

A Silly Little Ranch

By Todd R. Burns

A Silly Little Ranch

Ranch Boss Diana is Mom to all the animals who know

her voice and love her so.   They always say hello.

Especially when it's time to eat.

By Todd R. Burns

A Silly Little Ranch

About the author:

Todd is sometimes known as the old goat at A Silly

Little Ranch.

My favorite job at A Silly Little Ranch is to help tame

the animals so that everyone who visits can love and

enjoy them as much as we do.

By Todd R. Burns

A Silly Little Ranch

The Silly Little Ranch is an actual animal rescue and

petting zoo located in Marlow, Oklahoma and is open by

appointment on weekends.

Like and follow us on Facebook at DT Ranch

We hope to see you soon.

By Todd R. Burns

The

End

By Todd R. Burns

.

Made in the USA
Middletown, DE
18 April 2022

64411944R00038